Substitute Groundhog

Pat Miller

Illustrated by **Kathi Ember**

2012

FEB

Albert Whitman & Company, Morton Grove, Illinois

For Chris, Marty, and Bonnie,
and for the students at Sue Creech Elementary in Katy, Texas.
Now you have a book dedicated to you!—PM

To Breezy, for all his love and support over the years.—KE

Library of Congress Cataloging-in-Publication Data
Miller, Pat (Pat Glennda), 1951-
Substitute groundhog / by Pat Miller ; illustrated by Kathi Ember.
p. cm.
Summary: Too sick to perform his once-a-year job, Groundhog interviews other animals
to come out of his hole on Groundhog Day.
ISBN-13: 978-0-8075-7643-4 (hardcover)
ISBN-10: 0-8075-7643-3 (hardcover)
ISBN-13: 978-0-8075-7644-1 (paperback)
[1. Woodchuck—Fiction. 2. Groundhog Day—Fiction. 3. Armadillos—Fiction. 4. Animals—Habits and behavior—Fiction.]
I. Ember, Kathi, ill. II. Title.
PZ7.M63223Sub 2006 [E]—dc22 2006000113

The design is by Carol Gildar.

For information about Albert Whitman & Company,
please visit our web site at www.albertwhitman.com.

*T*he day before Groundhog Day, Groundhog
woke up sick. His muscles ached and his throat hurt.

Groundhog felt so awful he went to see Dr. Owl.

"You have a bad case of flu, you do," said Dr. Owl. "You need hot clover soup and bed rest for two days."

"*How* many?" asked Groundhog.

"Two, two," hooted Dr. Owl.

But Groundhog Day was tomorrow! Groundhog couldn't let everyone down because he was too sick to do his job. He tried to think of something.

Weather teller
Wanted
No experience needed
Apply at
Groundhog's Hole
February 1, 10:00 A.M.
Thanks,
Groundhog

On his way home to bed, Groundhog passed the Hidey Hole Diner. He saw want ads from all the neighborhood animals tacked to a nearby tree. Skunk was looking for a roommate. (Again.) Mr. and Mrs. Duck were returning north and had their nest for rent.

"I know what I'll do!" Groundhog thought. "I'll advertise for a substitute groundhog."

By ten o'clock, a line of animals waited to try out.
"Great!" said Groundhog with a sneeze. "Surely one of
you can do Groundhog Day for me."

Mole was first.

"You have to go down in my hole," Groundhog told Mole. "It's pretty dark down there."

"No problem," said Mole. "My own hole is even darker."

Mole got comfortable underground.

"Now come up and look for your shadow!" Groundhog shouted.

Mole peeked over the edge. His little eyes squinted.

"Well, Mole, what do you see?"

Mole spoke to a tree. "Is that you, Groundhog?"

Groundhog blew his nose. "This won't work. I need someone who sees well."

"I can see well!" said
a voice from high overhead.

Groundhog looked up
and saw Eagle.

Eagle swooped down. "From that mountain ledge, Groundhog, I could see a bit of owl feather stuck in your fur. I'd say you have been to Dr. Owl recently."

"Wow! Then surely you will have no trouble seeing your shadow," said Groundhog. "Climb down in the hole and let's practice."

"Climb down?" said Eagle. He looked at the entrance to the hole. "Will there be room down there to stretch my wings?" He stretched them wide. Very wide!

Groundhog rubbed his scratchy throat. "This won't work. I need someone who sees well and is not bothered by small spaces."

Bear stepped up next. "My own cave is snug and cozy."
"Great," said Groundhog. "Climb down and let's practice."
"This is perfect!" yelled Bear from the hole. "It's even more comfy than my own cave."

"Come out and take a look," called Groundhog.
There was no answer.

Groundhog poked his head below ground.
"Bear, come look for your shadow!"

The only answer was a deep, slow snore.

Groundhog was frustrated. He needed a substitute who could see well, wasn't bothered by small spaces, and wouldn't fall asleep.

"I can do it! I can do it! Let me try!"
Squirrel bounced to the front of the line.

"Okay," said Groundhog. "Go down
in the hole, come back up, and look for
your shadow."

Squirrel leaped in. "Wheee!"

Then she popped her head back up.
Groundhog said, "See your shadow?"
"Oh, I forgot to look!" Down she went.

She popped back up.
She dropped back down.
"I keep forgetting to look!"
Squirrel giggled. She popped up
and down some more.

"This is fun!"
she said.
But what Groundhog
needed was someone who would
pop up and *stay* up.

By now, Groundhog was feeling even worse. He thought of his warm bed. Was he ever going to find a substitute?

"Howdy there, Groundhog. How about giving me a chance?" Up stepped a strange-looking creature. "My name is Armadillo," she said.

"You're not from around here, are you?" asked Groundhog.

"Nope, I'm from Texas, visiting my cousin Badger," she said. "But I can do this job. I live in a hole. I like small spaces. I see my shadow just fine. And I will pop up and stay up."

Groundhog wasn't so sure. Armadillo was a stranger from far away. What did she know about the weather here? But she did have all the qualifications for the job.

"All right," said Groundhog. "Let's see how you do."

Armadillo climbed down into Groundhog's hole. She poked her head up and looked around. Sure enough, she saw her shadow.

"If that happens tomorrow, tell folks that winter will drag on," said Groundhog. "But if you don't see your shadow tomorrow, spring will come early."

"Got it," said Armadillo.

"I think you're just the substitute I've been looking for," said Groundhog. "You're hired!"

"Thanks," said Armadillo. They shook paws.

Then Groundhog climbed down his hole into bed. He sipped warm clover soup. He plumped his pillows and tucked his sore self under the flannel quilt.

The next morning, the animals gathered early to hear what Armadillo would say. It was cold and crisp as the sun peeked over the forest.

Badger served hot chocolate. Squirrel bounced and cheered for Armadillo. Eagle flew high above the trees. Muddy Mole looked sleepy and Bear was still in bed.

The animals grew quiet as Armadillo poked
her head up and carefully looked around. There on
the ground, she saw the shadow of her tiny ears
and pointy nose.

"Six more weeks of winter!" she announced.

Armadillo dropped back into Groundhog's hole.
"Did you hear that, Groundhog? Six more weeks of winter."
Groundhog groaned from his bed.
"How ya feeling, Groundhog?" Armadillo asked.

"A little better. But I'd feel a *lot* better if it was spring already," Groundhog said.

"Spring already?" said Armadillo. "Say, that gives me an idea."

Armadillo found Groundhog's suitcase.

"Get your gear together, Groundhog!" she said. "It's already spring in Texas! You can come home with me!"

"Really?" said Groundhog. He imagined himself rolling in warm grass instead of sneezing through six more weeks of cold.

"You bet," said Armadillo.

Groundhog jumped from his bed. He grabbed his teddy bear and his toothbrush and tossed them into his suitcase.

"I've always wanted to see Texas. Do you think they have cowboy hats in my size?" asked Groundhog.

"Sure as Texas has a Lone Star," said Armadillo. Together, they walked through the cold to the bus station.

And their shadows followed them all the way there.